ASTERIX
IN BRITAIN

TEXT BY GOSCINNY

DRAWINGS BY UDERZO

TRANSLATED BY ANTHEA BELL AND DEREK HOCKRIDGE

HODDER & STOUGHTON
LONDON LEICESTER SYDNEY AUCKLAND

PUBLISHERS OF ASTERIX IN OTHER LANGUAGES

Afrikaans	Human & Rousseau Publishers (Pty.) Ltd., State House, 3-9 Rose Street, Cape Town, S. Africa
Arabic	Dar El Maaref, 1119 Corniche El Nil, Cairo, Egypt
Basque *Galician*	Ediciones Jucar, Chantada 7, Madrid 29, Spain
Catalan *Valencian*	Ediciones Gaisa S.L., Avenida Marqués del Turia 67, Valencia, Spain
Brazilian	Cedibra, R. Filomena Nunes 162, Rio de Janeiro, Brazil
Danish	Gutenberghus Bladene, Vognmagergade 11, 1148 Copenhagen K, Denmark
Dutch	Amsterdam Boek, Witbautstraat 129, Amsterdam, Holland
English	Hodder & Stoughton, Arlen House, Salisbury Road, Leicester LE1 7QS, England
Finnish	Sanoma Osakeyhtio, Ludviginkatu 2-10, 00130 Helsinki 13, Finland
Flemish	Editions du Lombard, Avenue P.-H., Spaak 1-11, Brussels 7, Belgium
German	Delta Verlag, Postfach 1215, 7 Stuttgart 1, West Germany
Icelandic	Fjolvi HF, Raudalak 20, Reykjavik, Iceland
Italian	Arnoldo Mondadori Editore, Via Bianca de Savoia 20, 20122, Milan, Italy
Latin	Delta Verlag, Postfach 1215, 7 Stuttgart 1, West Germany
Norwegian	A/S Hjemmet, Christian den 4des Gate 13, Oslo 1, Norway
Persian	Editions Universelles, Modern Printing House, Avenue Ekbatan, Teheran, Iran
Portuguese	Livreria Bertrand, Rua Joao de Deus-Venda Nova, Amadora, Portugal
Serbo-Croat	Nip Forum, Vojvode Misica 1-3, 21000 Novi Sad, Jugoslavia
Spanish	Editorial Abril, Avenida Leandro N. Alem 896, Buenos Aires, Argentina
Spanish	Editorial Bruguera, Camps y Fabrés 5, Barcelona 6, Spain
Swedish	Hemmets Journal, Fack 200 22 Malmo, Sweden
Turkish	Kervan Kitabcilik, Serefendi Sokagi 31, Cagaloglu — Istanbul, Turkey

Affiliates of Dargaud Editeur
Dargaud Canada Ltée, 300 Place d'Youville, Montreal 125, Québec, Canada
Dargaud Benelux, 3 Rue Kindermans, 1050 Brussels, Belgium
Interpress S.A., En Budron B, 1052 Le Mont/Lausanne, Switzerland

ISBN 0 340 10388 4 (cased edition)
ISBN 0 340 17221 5 (paperbound edition)

Copyright © 1966 Dargaud Editeur
English-language text copyright © 1970 Hodder & Stoughton Ltd

First published in Great Britain in 1970 (cased) by
Brockhampton Press Ltd (now Hodder and Stoughton Children's Books),
Salisbury Road, Leicester
First published in Great Britain in 1973 (paperbound)

8 9 10 11 (cased edition)
5 6 7 8 (paperbound edition)

Printed in Belgium by Henri Proost & Cie, Turnhout

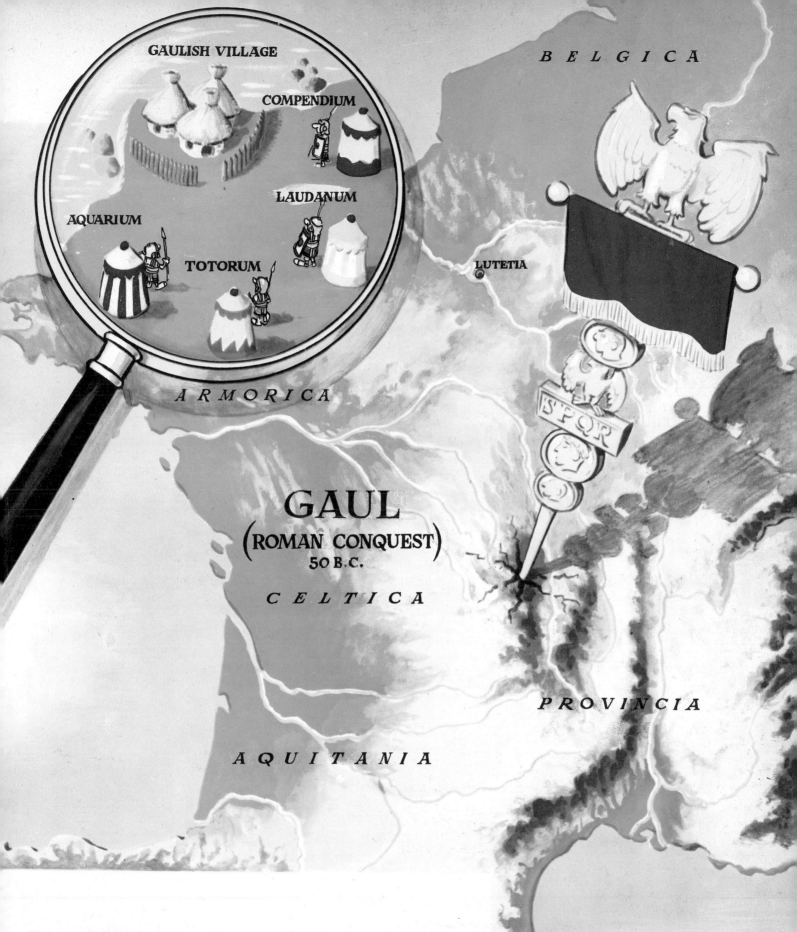

GAULISH VILLAGE

COMPENDIUM

LAUDANUM

AQUARIUM

TOTORUM

ARMORICA

BELGICA

LUTETIA

SPQR

GAUL
(ROMAN CONQUEST)
50 B.C.

CELTICA

PROVINCIA

AQUITANIA

The year is 50 BC. Gaul is entirely occupied by the Romans. Well, not entirely… One small village of indomitable Gauls still holds out against the invaders. And life is not easy for the Roman legionaries who garrison the fortified camps of Totorum, Aquarium, Laudanum and Compendium…

a few of the Gauls

Asterix, the hero of these adventures. A shrewd, cunning little warrior; all perilous missions are immediately entrusted to him. Asterix gets his superhuman strength from the magic potion brewed by the druid Getafix...

Obelix, Asterix's inseparable friend. A menhir delivery-man by trade; addicted to wild boar. Obelix is always ready to drop everything and go off on a new adventure with Asterix – so long as there's wild boar to eat, and plenty of fighting.

Getafix, the venerable village druid. Gathers mistletoe and brews magic potions. His speciality is the potion which gives the drinker superhuman strength. But Getafix also has other recipes up his sleeve...

Cacofonix, the bard. Opinion is divided as to his musical gifts. Cacofonix thinks he's a genius. Everyone else thinks he's unspeakable. But so long as he doesn't speak, let alone sing, everybody likes him...

Finally, Vitalstatistix, the chief of the tribe. Majestic, brave and hot-tempered, the old warrior is respected by his men and feared by his enemies. Vitalstatistix himself has only one fear; he is afraid the sky may fall on his head tomorrow. But as he always says, 'Tomorrow never comes.'

5

9

13

16

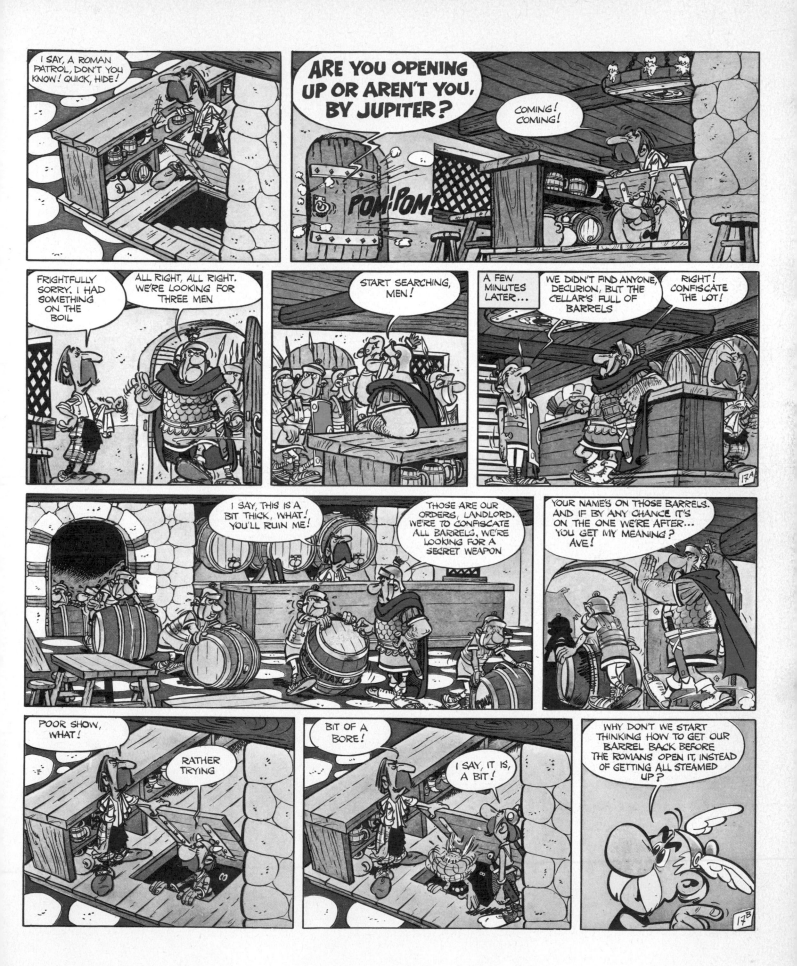

21

25

35

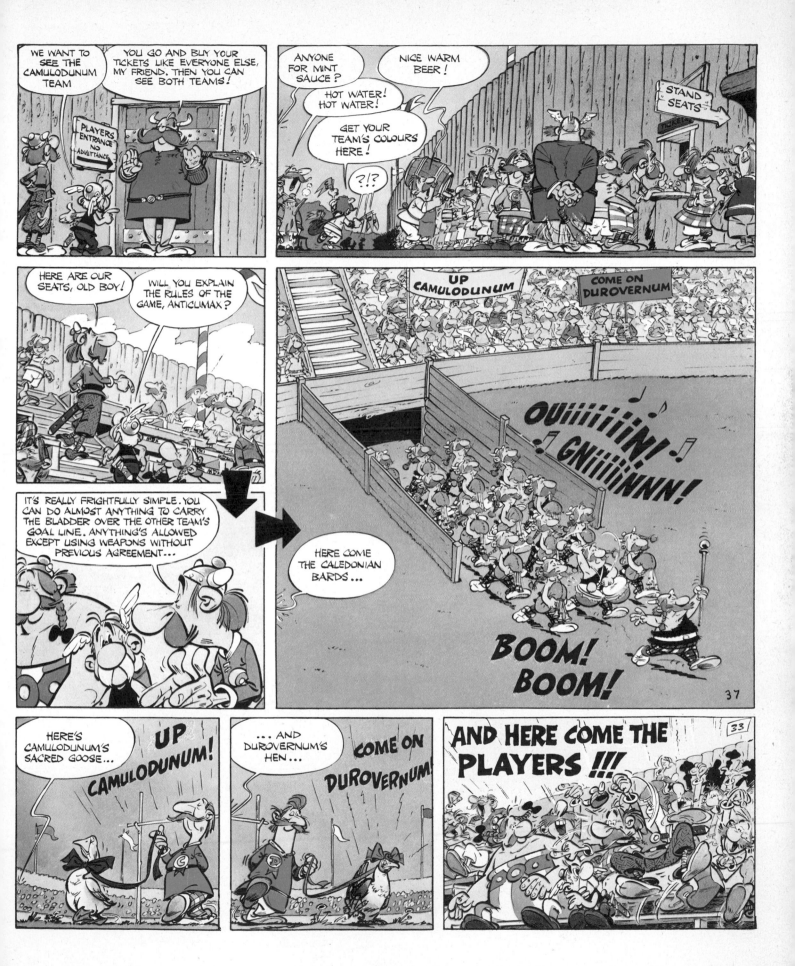

39

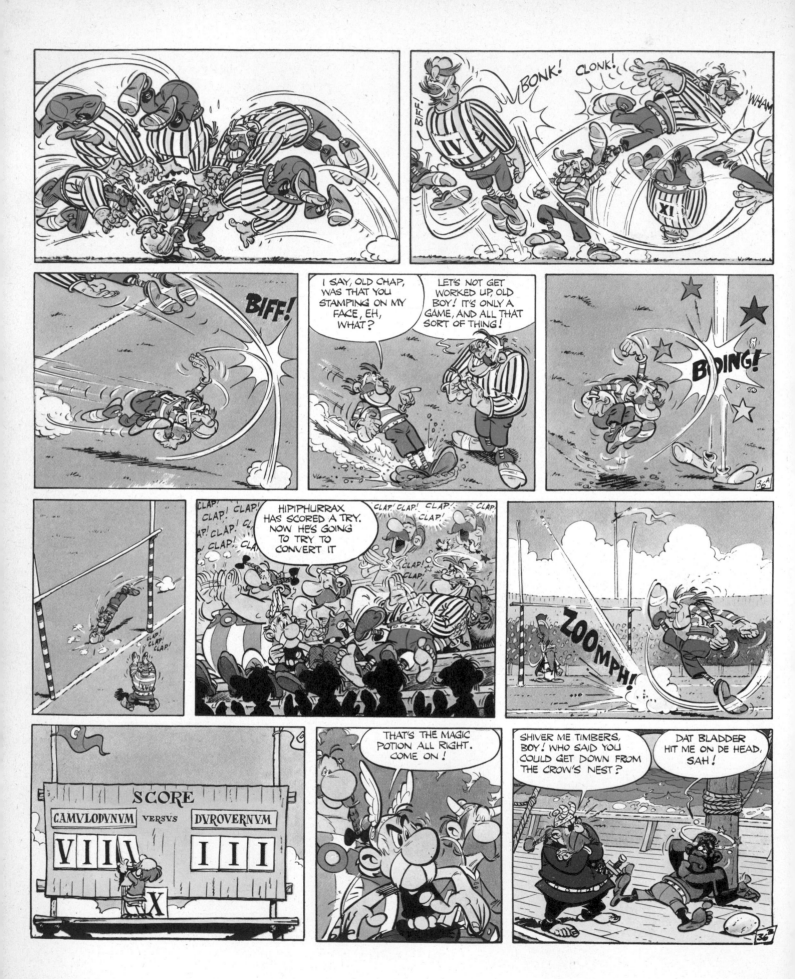

41

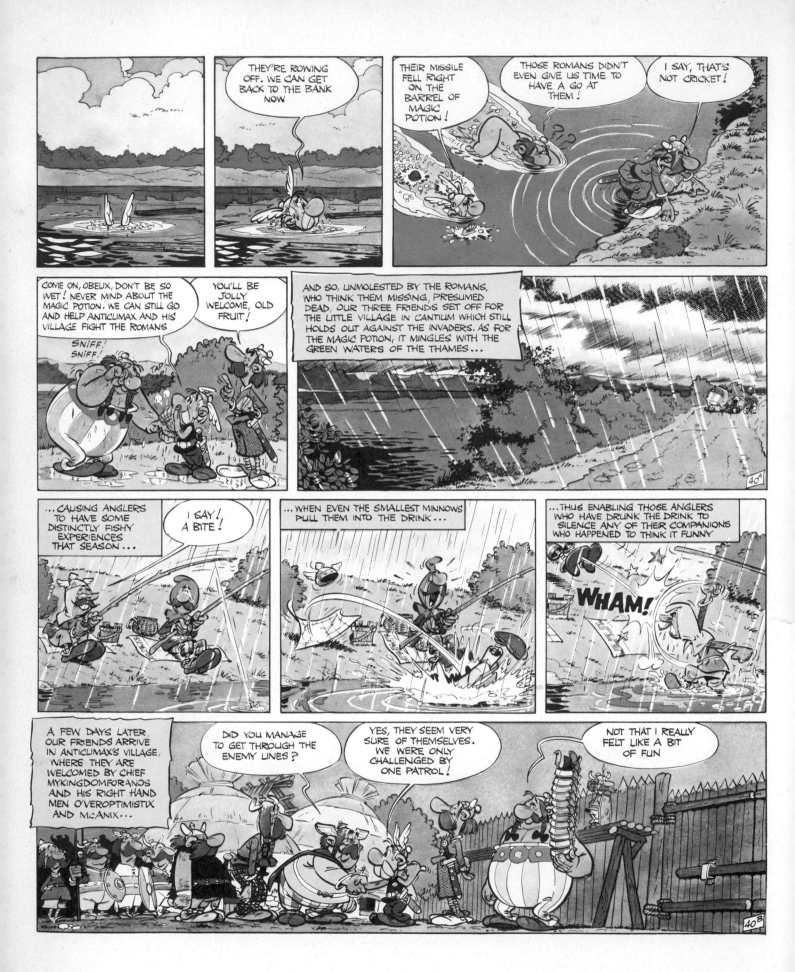

proost Turnhout (Belgium)

PRINTED IN BELGIUM